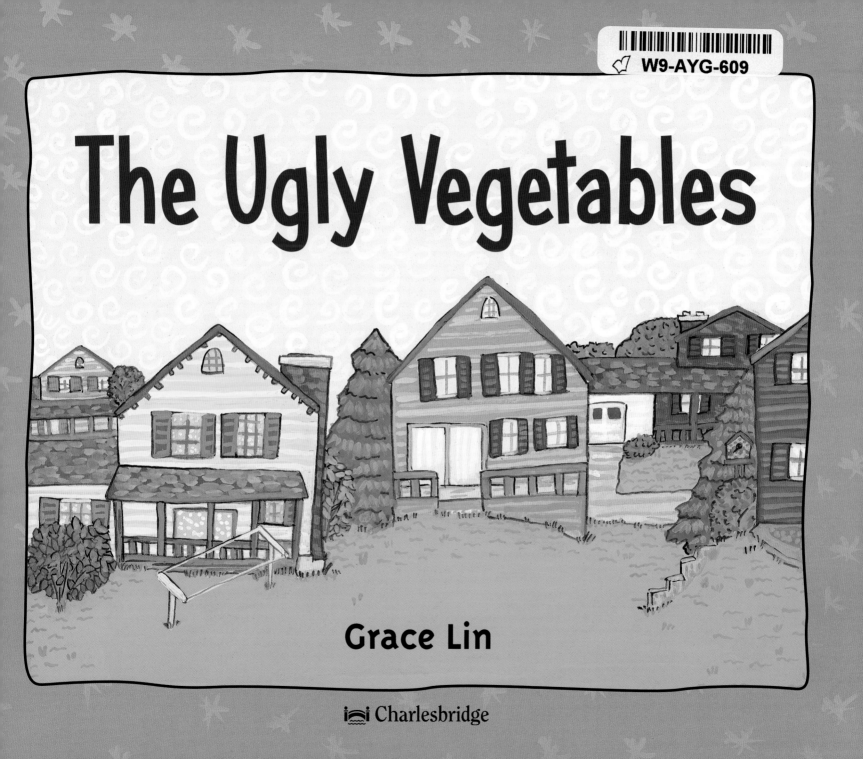

The Ugly Vegetables

Grace Lin

Charlesbridge

Text and illustrations copyright © 1999 by Grace Lin
Jacket and border illustrations copyright © 2009 by Grace Lin

Published by Charlesbridge
85 Main Street, Watertown, MA 02472
(617) 926-0329
www.charlesbridge.com

Illustrations done in gouache on Canson watercolor paper
Display type and text type set in Candy Square and Triplex
Color separations by Chroma Graphics, Singapore
Printed and bound February 2013 by Regent Publishing
Services in ShenZhen, Guangdong, China
Production supervision by Brian G. Walker
Designed by Diane M. Earley and Susan Mallory Sherman

Library of Congress Cataloging-in-Publication Data
Lin, Grace
  The ugly vegetables / Grace Lin.
     p.   cm
  Summary: A little girl thinks her mother's garden is the
ugliest in the neighborhood until she discovers that flowers
might look and smell pretty but Chinese vegetable soup
smells best of all. Includes a recipe.
ISBN: 978-0-88106-336-3 (reinforced for library use)
ISBN: 978-1-57091-491-1 (softcover)
[1. Vegetables, Chinese—Fiction. 2. Gardens—Fiction.
3. Chinese Americans—Fiction.] I. Title.
PZ7.L644Ug   1999
[E]—dc21   98-26863

Printed in China
(hc) 10 9 8 7 6 5 4
(sc) 10 9 8

For my mom and her ugly gardens

—G. L.

A note to the reader:
You may find some unfamiliar words
in this story. Pronounce them as you guess
they sound from the way they are spelled,
or turn to the last page of the book for help.

In the spring I helped my mother start our garden. We used tall shovels to turn the grass upside down, and I saw pink worms wriggle around. It was hard work. When we stopped to rest, we saw that the neighbors were starting their gardens, too.

"Hello, Irma!" my mother called to Mrs. Crumerine. Mrs. Crumerine was digging, too. She was using a small shovel, one that fit in her hand.

"Mommy," I asked, "why are we using such big shovels? Mrs. Crumerine has a small one."

"Because our garden needs more digging," she said.

I helped my mother plant the seeds, and we dragged the hose to the garden.

"Hi, Linda! Hi, Mickey!" I called to the Fitzgeralds. They were sprinkling water on their garden with green watering cans.

"Mommy," I asked, "why are we using a hose? Linda and Mickey use watering cans."

"Because our garden needs more water," she said.

Then my mother drew funny pictures on pieces of paper, and I stuck them into the garden.

"Hello, Roseanne!" my mother called across the street to Mrs. Angelhowe.

"Mommy," I asked, "why are we sticking these papers in the garden? Mrs. Angelhowe has seed packages in her garden."

"Because our garden is going to grow Chinese vegetables," she told me. "These are the names of the vegetables in Chinese, so I can tell which plants are growing where."

One day I saw our garden growing. Little green stems that looked like grass had popped out from the ground.

"Our garden's growing!" I yelled. "Our garden's growing!"

I rushed over to the neighbors' gardens to see if theirs had grown. Their plants looked like little leaves.

"Mommy," I asked, "why do our plants look like grass? The neighbors' plants look different."

"Because they are growing flowers," she said.

"Why can't we grow flowers?" I asked.

"These are better than flowers," she said.

Soon all the neighbors' gardens were blooming. Up and down
the street grew rainbows of flowers.

The wind always smelled sweet, and butterflies and bees flew everywhere. Everyone's garden was beautiful, except for ours.

Our garden was all dark green and ugly.

"Why didn't we grow flowers?" I asked again.

"These are better than flowers," Mommy said again.

I looked, but saw only black-purple-green vines, fuzzy wrinkled leaves, prickly stems, and a few little yellow flowers.

"I don't think so," I said.

"You wait and see," Mommy said.

Before long, our vegetables grew. Some were big and lumpy. Some were thin and green and covered with bumps. Some were just plain icky yellow. They were ugly vegetables.

Sometimes I would go over to the neighbors' and look at their pretty gardens. They would show the poppies and peonies and petunias to me, and I would feel sad that our garden wasn't as nice.

One day my mother and I picked the vegetables from the garden.
We filled a whole wheelbarrow full of them. We wheeled them to the
kitchen. My mother washed them, took a big knife, and started
to chop them.

"Aie-yow!" she said when she cut them. She had to use all her muscles.
The vegetables were hard and tough.

"This is a xĭao hú gūa," Mommy said, handing me a bumpy,
curled vegetable. She pointed at the other vegetables. "This is xìan cài.
That's a tóng hāo."

I went outside to play. While I was playing catch with Mickey, a magical aroma filled the air. I saw the neighbors standing on their porches with their eyes closed, smelling the sky. They took deep breaths of air, like they were trying to eat the smell.

The wind carried it up and down the street. Even the bees and the butterflies seemed to smell the scent in the breeze.

I smelled it too. It made me hungry, and it was coming from my house!

When I followed the smell to my house, my mother was putting a big bowl of soup on the table. The soup was yellow and red and green and pink.

"This is a special soup," Mommy said, and she smiled.

She gave me a small bowl full of it, and I tasted it. It was so good! The flavors of the soup seemed to dance in my mouth and laugh all the way down to my stomach. I smiled.

"Do you like it?" Mommy asked me.

I nodded and held out my bowl for some more.

"It's made from our vegetables," she told me.

Then the doorbell rang, and we ran to open the door.

All our neighbors were standing at the door holding flowers.

"We noticed you were cooking." Mr. Fitzgerald laughed as he held out his flowers. "We thought maybe you might be interested in a trade!"

We laughed, too, and my mother gave them each their own bowl of her special soup.

My mother told them what each vegetable was and how she grew it. She gave them the soup recipe and put some soup into jars for them to take home. I ate five bowls of soup.

It was the best dinner ever.

The next spring, when my mother was starting her garden,
we planted some flowers next to the Chinese vegetables.
Mrs. Crumerine, the Fitzgeralds, and the Angelhowes planted some
Chinese vegetables next to their flowers.

Soon the whole neighborhood was growing Chinese vegetables in their
gardens. Up and down the street, little green plants poked out of the
ground. Some looked like leaves and some looked like grass, and when
the flowers started blooming, you could smell soup in the air.

The Ugly Vegetables

菜   cài (zai) — This symbol emphasizes that the word refers to a vegetable.

空心菜   kōng xīn cài (kung shin zai) — This literally means "hollow heart vegetable." The stem is hollow, like a tube.

莧菜   xìan cài (shen zai) — This is a red-lined, red-rimmed vegetable.

艽菜   jǐu cài (joe zai) — Also called Chinese leeks, these look like blades of grass.

茼蒿   tóng hāo (tung how) — These have chrysanthemum-like flowers and edible leaves.

小胡瓜   xǐao hú gūa (show hwang gwa) — Also called Chinese cucumbers, these are long, thin, and covered with bumps.

絲瓜   sī gūa (see gwa) — The inside of this vegetable is spongy-looking. It tastes best when it is fresh.

苦瓜   kǔ gūa (coo gwa) — The Chinese means "bitter melon." It is brightly colored, bumpy, and bittersweet.

葫蘆瓠   hū lú hù (foo loo foo) — These are pale yellow gourds that are used for decoration.

Ugly Vegetable Soup

Ingredients:
1 can chicken broth
1 can water
5 dried scallops
4-oz. piece of chicken
cornstarch
1/2 cup chopped xǐao hú gūa
1 cup chopped sī gūa
1 cup tóng hāo
1 cup xìan cài
1 cup kōng xīn cài
pepper

Directions:
Bring chicken broth, water, and scallops to a boil in a large pot. While waiting, cut chicken into bite-size pieces and coat them with cornstarch. Wash all vegetables. When broth starts to boil, put in the chicken pieces, one by one. When the chicken begins to look cooked, add chopped xǐao hú gūa and sī gūa. Turn heat to low and let soup simmer for about 10 minutes. Then bring the soup to a high boil. Quickly add the tóng hāo, xìan cài, and kōng xīn cài and let them boil for 1 minute. Add pepper to taste and serve! Serves 5.